This book is dedicated to:
My loves, Nicole and Noah,
my parents and sisters,
and HCL 6.

"Courage is the most important of all the
virtues because without courage, you can't
practice any other virtue consistently."
-Maya Angelou

www.mascotbooks.com

Little Benny Piggy in Courage for the Win

For more information, please contact:
Mascot Books
620 Herndon Parkway #320
Herndon, VA 20170
info@mascotbooks.com

Library of Congress Control Number: 2019906816

CPSIA Code: PRT0719A
ISBN-13: 978-1-64543-169-5

Printed in the United States

Little Benny Piggy in
Courage for the Win

Written by Ben Stein
Illustrated by
Natia Gogiashvili & Ben Stein

Little Benny Piggy was lonely at home
so he decided to go to the park and roam.

He wanted to play and have fun
and run around free in the sun.

But when he got there he felt a scare
because he didn't know anyone there.

He thought, *They don't want to play with me so I guess I'll just sit alone by this tree.*

Then a squirrel scurried to him named Savant
and asked Benny, "What do you want?"

He said, "I want to fit in
and have friends I love like kin."

"But I am different and fat
and not very good when up to bat."

Savant thought for a minute and said,
"Here's some wisdom for your heart and head."

"To make friends just be you
and whatever you fear just do.

Feel the fear and say,
'I would like to play.'"

"They'll see you as a piggy brave
and your friendship they'll crave."

Benny wanted to hide, but took a stand
with the intention of a pig with command.

He said to the pitcher, "I play with heart."
And the pitcher replied, "Next inning you can start."

Little Benny Piggy smiled ear to ear
as his new teammates gave him a cheer.

"Little Benny Piggy hooray!
Making you as a new friend made our day!"

Little Benny Piggy felt grateful and proud
of the gift of courage he had found.

About the Author

Ben Stein is a life and career coach who is passionate about helping people design their ideal life with purpose, courage, and intention at Purpose Up. He is also a dad blogger at IHopeIDon'tKillIt.com.

In past lives, he's been an award winning advertising producer, product manager, and world traveler. He currently resides in Miami, Florida with his wife and son.

www.littlebennypiggy.com